W9-BHU-440

WHEN CHILDREN PLAY
The Story of RIGHT TO PLAY

Gina McMurchy-Barber

Fitzhenry & Whiteside

Text copyright © 2013 Gina McMurchy-Barber

Published in Canada by Fitzhenry & Whiteside, 195 Allstate Parkway, Markham, Ontario L3R 4T8

Published in the United States by Fitzhenry & Whiteside, 311 Washington Street, Brighton, Massachusetts 02135

All rights reserved. No part of this book may be reproduced in any manner without the express written consent of the publisher, except in the case of brief excerpts in critical reviews and articles. All inquiries should be addressed to Fitzhenry & Whiteside Limited, 195 Allstate Parkway, Markham, Ontario L3R 4T8.

www.fitzhenry.ca   godwit@fitzhenry.ca

10 9 8 7 6 5 4 3 2 1

Library and Archives Canada Cataloguing in Publication

McMurchy-Barber, Gina

When children play : the story of Right To Play / Gina McMurchy-Barber.

ISBN 978-1-55455-154-5

1. Right To Play International--History--Juvenile
literature. 2. Outdoor recreation for children--Social
aspects--Juvenile literature. 3. Sports for children--Social
aspects--Juvenile literature. 4. Play--Social aspects--Juvenile
literature. I. Title.

GV191.63.M35 2011   j306.481   C2011-901396-7

Publisher Cataloging-in-Publication Data (U.S.)

McMurchy-Barber, Gina.

When children play : the story of Right To Play / Gina McMurchy-Barber.

[56] p. : col. photos. ; cm.

Summary: A history of Right To Play and their role to improve the lives of children in some of the most disadvantaged areas of the world by using the power of sport and play for development, health and peace.

ISBN: 978-1-55455-154-5 (pbk.)

1. Right To Play International – History – Juvenile literature. 2. Outdoor recreation for children – Social aspects – Juvenile literature. 3. Sports for children – Social aspects – Juvenile literature. 4. Play – Social aspects – Juvenile literature. I. Title.

306.481 dc22 GV191.63.M33 2013

Fitzhenry & Whiteside acknowledges with thanks the Canada Council for the Arts, and the Ontario Arts Council for their support of our publishing program. We acknowledge the financial support of the Government of Canada through the Canada Book Fund (CBF) for our publishing activities.

Cover and interior design by Daniel Choi

Cover image courtesy of: Right To Play

Printed in China by Sheck Wah Tong Printing Press Ltd.

For Nathan and Cameron—who never missed a chance to play.

Grateful acknowledgements go to Julia Myer for being a source of valuable information, and to Robin Cowie, John Nsabimana, Mohamad Assaf and Coach Dean Cantelon for sharing their experiences. I also want to thank Christie Harkin for her determination to seeing this book come to life and Solange Messier for her insightful editing of my manuscript.

FEB 0 9 2015

Contents

Chapter 1   6

Let's Play

Chapter 2   12

How the Red Ball Got Rolling

Chapter 3   24

The Right To Play Team

Chapter 4   36

Playing the Game

Chapter 5   44

A Team Anyone Can Join

Chapter 6   50

Becoming a Team Member

Glossary   54

Index   55

Resources   56

References   56

Credit Right To Play

This young girl (left) has many family responsibilities and few opportunities to play. Thanks to Right to Play, these girls (right) are learning the joy of playing cooperative games.

Chapter 1

Let's Play

Have you ever felt down, bored or lonely, but then a friend came along and said, "Hey, you want to play?" Maybe you had a game of catch, kicked a ball around, or played hide and seek. Whatever it was, it probably didn't take long before you forgot your worries and felt full of energy, enthusiasm and joy. That's no surprise because play has a magical way of making us feel happy and good about ourselves.

Some people—you know, the ones they call *experts*—say play is the most important work a kid can do. That's right! Not only is play fun and good exercise, it's also a way for kids to learn about sharing, negotiating and compromising, improvising and inventing, acting with grace and sportsmanship, and making goals and mastering challenges. Not only that, play can improve a child's self-esteem and help heal painful memories too.

Oh yeah. One other great thing about play: It gives children the opportunity to become key players in a worldwide peace movement. Play puts everyone on an even playing field where the focus is on the game, on playing it well, and on making it fun for everyone. Religion, race, nationality, gender, and physical ability do not matter. Play removes barriers and builds on our common need to express joy in movement.

Play is so important for healthy development that the **United Nations (UN)** created an international agreement, the **UN Convention on the Rights of the Child, Article 31,** that states every child has the right to engage in play and recreational activities and that their governments must respect, promote and protect this right. Many world leaders understand that protecting children's right to play is a great way to raise healthy, caring and responsible citizens.

Unfortunately, even with this special UN agreement in place, there are many children around the world who never get the chance to play. Sometimes it's because their countries have been at war, or they face extreme poverty or disease. Some children who are forced to become soldiers lose the ability to be childlike and joyful and can't forget the horrors they have seen or forgive themselves for participating in war. Others never learn to play because they have to work long hours in hot factories or out in the fields.

Some have to take on the role of parenting their younger brothers and sisters. In some regions, certain children aren't allowed to play simply because they are girls or have physical disabilities.

It's for them, the world's most disadvantaged children, that Right To Play was started. For over a decade now, this humanitarian organization has been helping to bring laughter and smiles to children all around the world. It uses sports and play to educate, improve health, and build confident youth who want to give back to their communities.

Along with thousands of their famous red soccer balls and other sports equipment, Right To Play sets up programs, mentors youth, and educates for peace and health with the help of thousands of volunteers. Local coaches, teachers and professional athletes form an international team of players whose goal it is to see that every child has the right to play. They've seen first-hand that when children play, the world wins.

A chance to play opens up new possibilities for these children in Umphium Refugee Camp, Thailand.

Credit Right To Play

Cole's Story: A Game Where Everyone Wins

Cole Cantelon and his teammates stared out the window of their bus as it made its way through the slums just north of Uganda's capital, Kampala. Back home in Canada, these 11- to 13-year-old boys had all seen pictures of places like this before, but it was nothing compared to actually being there. The rows upon rows of little shacks pieced together with scraps of wood, brick and mud made the garden sheds in their backyards look like palaces. And even if a murder of opportunist crows tipped over every garbage can in their neighbourhoods and scattered the contents far and wide, it would never look like the garbage they saw.

What about all the barefooted children— why weren't they in school or playing in their yards or being watched over by parents?

The team soon arrived at the only full-size Little League baseball field in Uganda. As they began to trickle out of the bus and into the sticky heat of the typical Ugandan January day, it hit them—they were finally going to meet the team they were supposed to face five months earlier at the 2011 Little League World Series in Williamsport, Pennsylvania. Both teams were champions, each having won their way to representing their regions at this international event, but

Credit: Pamela Cantelon

Cole and his new friend Gingo.

"When Children Play, The World Wins." This motto was never truer than when these two Little League teams came together to play baseball in January 2012

in the end only the Canadians actually got to go.

The Ugandan boys could not play at the World Series because they did not have proper identification to enter the United States. In Uganda, it is not unusual for a child to have no birth certificate or other identifying paperwork. Sometimes it's because his mom and dad cannot read and write, other times, it is because he's being raised by foster parents who do not know the details of his birth and family.

"We felt bad for them," remembered Cole, pitcher and third baseman for the Canadians. "I know how I'd feel if it was our team that wasn't allowed to go to the World Series."

Like wildfire, the unfortunate news spread around the world. One heartfelt protest came from Ruth Hoffman, a businesswoman who lives in Vancouver, British Columbia. Soon there was a flurry of calls and emails between Ruth and organizers from Right To Play. They all agreed that something had to be done.

With Right To Play's backing, generous donations started arriving and in no time at all there was enough money to send the Canadian Little Leaguers to Uganda. Even better, they had enough funds to build the kids in Kampala's slums a new multi-purpose playing field where both boys and girls would have a chance to play baseball, softball and other kinds of sports.

"Their lives are so different from ours," Cole said, thinking of the slums where his new friends lived. "But they don't see what they have as being so bad—they're very proud of their lives and where they live. That's nice to see."

Now, months later, the Canadian and Ugandan Little League teams finally had their chance to face each other on the ball field— like they were meant to at the World Series. As Cole and his teammates crossed the field, they were met with wide grins and hearty handshakes from the likes of Ivan Luyombya, Solomon Gingo, and Abooki Barugahare, a few of the top players on Uganda's team. Looking on from the sidelines were dozens of parents and friends from both teams, and lots of reporters and photographers from many of the world's biggest news sources. Some pretty famous ball players were there too—like Gregg Zaun, former catcher of the Toronto Blue Jays and Right To Play Athlete Ambassador. There's no doubt that it was the biggest crowd to ever attend a game in the history of Uganda's Little League Baseball.

For players like Ivan, Gingo and Abooki, baseball was their reason for living and their chance to get out of the slums—even if it was just for a few hours a day. They were eager to get the game started and to show the Canadians and the world what they could do.

As for the Canadians, they were just as keen to get going. They had flown thousands of miles to be there and though they got their chance to play at the World Series, this was the team they were supposed to play first.

The game was anything but uneventful, but by the end of the fifth inning, the score stood at Uganda 1, Canada 0. Then, at the top of the sixth and final inning, the Canadians got their chance and Cole Cantelon scored the run that tied up the game. For anyone watching, the end seemed certain, but then again Uganda still had last bats. Moments later a loud chorus of celebration rang out as the smallest player on Uganda's team, Felix Aboki, was walked across home plate for the win.

That night, as Cole and the rest of the Canadian team made their way back to the hotel with the excitement of the day still fresh in their minds, they passed through the slums again. With the sun fast setting on Uganda, they noticed there was no electricity in the dimly lit shacks. Only candlelight and lanterns cast flickering shadows on the walls. Not far away, sitting in their own poorly lit homes, were the boys from the Ugandan team. Only tonight, the glow on their faces was enough to light any room. For them, the 2–1 victory over Canada was sweet and well-earned. For the Canadians, defeat was also sweet, for there could never really be any losers in a game such as this one.

"We didn't feel bad at all," Cole explained. "It was great seeing them—how they were when they won. They ran to the outfield, laughing and cheering—and so did we."

Here's a Game to Try: Batter Up

What you'll need:

- Tennis racquet or large plastic bat
- Tennis ball, rubber ball, or dense foam ball
- This game is best with a minimum of six players

Instructions:

1. Decide the boundaries of the play area.
2. One player is batter and the others are outfield.
3. The batter hits the ball to the outfield where someone tries to catch it.
4. The batter then places the racquet or bat on the ground facing the other players.
5. The player who catches the ball gets one point. He can make an additional two points by rolling the ball on the ground and hitting the racquet or bat with it.
6. The player who gets five points first trades places with the batter and the game continues as before.

Results:

The beauty of this game is it requires very little equipment. It can even be played with just a large ball (such as a soccer or rubber ball) and a stick from the forest. The only difference would be that the batter kicks the ball out to the fielders and the one who catches will try hitting the stick.

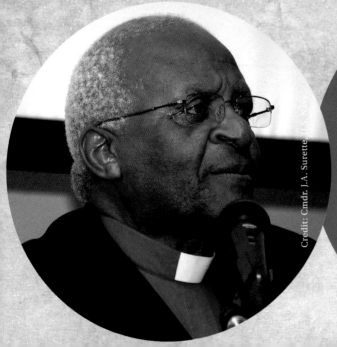

Credit: Cmdr. J.A. Surette, U.S. Navy

"Children who were enemies are becoming friends, and sport is helping the process of reconciliation and helping the wounded and traumatized mend. Quite clearly, sport, and all those who assist in this process, will help us overcome disease, ignorance and poverty."

Archbishop Desmond Tutu, Nobel Peace Prize recipient and champion for human rights worldwide

Credit: Right To Play

Nothing could be more fun than a shiny new ball and a game with friends.

Chapter 2

How the Red Ball Got Rolling

A long time ago, members of the Lille-hammer Olympic Organizing Com-mittee **(LOOC)** were busy prepar-ing for the upcoming 1994 Winter Olympics about to be held in Lillehammer, Norway. There were things to make—jumps, moguls, and courses for the skiers; icy tracks for the bobsled and luge teams; and new rinks and racing ovals for the figure skaters and speed skaters. There were also events to plan, and people to organize. The city had to be upgrad-ed too, to make sure it could handle all the athletes and tourists coming to Lillehammer to participate in one of the world's largest in-ternational events—the XVII Winter Olympic Games.

Not far from that quiet little city, people in Eastern Europe were in the midst of a different kind of event—a devastating war in the former Federal Republic of Yugoslavia. At that same time, millions of people in Africa and Asia were facing famines, natural disasters, and conflicts that were destroying lives, homes, and peace of mind. All these international emergencies cast a shadow over the world and the upcoming Winter Olympics.

Members of the organizing committee continued preparing for the big event, while at the same time, looking for a way to support those facing terrible challenges. Their response needed to be connected to the Olympics in a way that would honour the value and potential of sports. The solution was to use sports and play to improve the lives of suffering children and their communities. But who could they turn to for help and how would they do it? The answer was easy—they would tap into the energy and enthusiasm of their Olympic athletes. The athletes would be the face of the organization and help raise funds before, during and after the Games.

In 1992, **Olympic Aid** was born. A budding, non-profit humanitarian organization, Olympic Aid provided athletes with the opportunity to use their talents to do more than win medals. It gave them a chance to change the world.

The Olympic Aid Team

Every successful team needs great players: That's what the Lillehammer Olympic Organizing Committee was thinking when it set out to find the first Olympic Aid team. The athletes chosen would have to be willing to raise funds and ensure the money found its way to children and families in distress through Olympic Aid's partners—the Red Cross, Save the Children and other smaller Norwegian non-profit organizations.

To get the ball rolling, the LOOC chose five Norwegian Winter Olympians for the job. Cato Zahl Pedersen is a Paralympics downhill skier who won thirteen gold medals and one silver medal in the 1994 Games. Trude Dybendahl and Vegard Ulvang are both cross-country skiers. Trude won a silver medal in the 1994 Games while Vegard won three gold medals. Retired athlete Hjalmar Andersen was the only three-time gold-medal winner in men's speed skating at the 1952 Oslo Winter Olympics. These four Olympic Aid ambassadors had the immediate job of letting the world know about this new charitable branch of the Olympic Games, and then inspiring people to donate money to the cause.

Norway's top speed skater and four-time gold medalist Johann Olav Koss was Olympic

Playing games can teach kids to think creatively and cooperatively. Students from Ban Pluckwa School in Satun, Thailand, show a new way to share the ball.

Credit: Right To Play

Credit: Cliff

Johann Olav Koss skated to victory and a gold medal, just days after surgery.

just five days after pancreatic surgery. That kind of determination and stamina proved Johann was an unstoppable young man—and just the kind of person Olympic Aid needed to lead the organization.

In 1993, Johann's first act as Olympic Aid ambassador was to visit the little war-weary country of Eritrea in East Africa. He had visited Africa before so he had some idea of what to expect. But nothing he had ever seen could have prepared him for the devastation Eritrea faced after thirty years of warring with neighbouring Ethiopia. As Johann visited one refugee camp after another, he saw the sad faces of poverty, sickness, and despair. Remarkably, he also found tiny flickers of hope as he went about meeting the Eritreans.

One morning, when the temperature was already soaring above 30°C (86°F), Johann was visiting one of the many slums in and around the capital of Asmara. He had a gift, but he didn't know who to give it to. Should it be given to one of the many beggars or the overburdened mother with three children clinging to her body? Maybe the gift should go to the little girl with the dusty hair and sunken cheeks. Then Johann spotted two boys lounging by the side of the road. Like most of the children he had seen that day, they were thin and dirty, and wore faded and tattered t-shirts.

Johann stooped down and asked the boys, "Do you like to play?" Suddenly their dull little faces lit up.

"We like to play football." They grinned and then pointed across the street. "But only when our friend Saleh Abraha is around." Johann looked across the way at an ordinary nine-year-old boy and wondered what unique talent he possessed to make him so

Aid's fifth team player. Johann threw himself into the job with his whole heart and soon stood out as the one person who could lead Olympic Aid long after the Lillehammer Winter Olympic Games were over. He not only excelled in his sport, but also showed leadership skills and a genuine desire to improve the lives of the world's most disadvantaged children. He quickly became Olympic Aid's team captain.

Johann Olav Koss

During the 1992 Winter Olympics in Albertville, France, Johann won the men's speed skating gold and silver medals in the 1,500m and 10,000m races. But that's not what made the Olympic officials, the press, and the public sit up and pay attention. What made everyone's jaw drop was how he competed

Credit: Right To Play

Johann knows that play can be more than just having fun — it's a way to teach.

Johann Olav Koss was born on October 29, 1968 in Oslo, Norway. Since childhood, Johann loved skating, though at first he was not very good at it. But he was willing to work hard, and even after failing to qualify for the Norwegian team in 1988, he pressed on until he won a place on the team in 1992. He was later asked to assistant-coach the Norwegian national speed skating team for the 2010 Winter Olympics in Vancouver, British Columbia.

important to his two friends. Maybe he was a great football player, he thought, or had a special gift for organizing the children. The only thing unusual Johann noticed, as he wiped the sweat from his brow, was that the boy wore a long-sleeved shirt.

As Johann watched, it soon became obvious what made Saleh Abraha so popular with his friends. All three boys removed their shirts and bunched them together. With Saleh's long sleeves wound around the others and tied into a knot, those rags were transformed into a tight ball. The hot and dusty street suddenly came to life as the three boys kicked and passed their homemade shirt-ball back and forth. Johann had never seen such joy over something so simple; it made him laugh deep

in his belly. Now he knew who he should give his gift to.

Out of his bag, Johann pulled a shiny new soccer ball. As he handed it over, he couldn't help smiling at the boys' astonished faces. "This is for you...and when I come again it will be with more sports equipment."

Johann's small encounter with three young strangers left a deep impression on him. He returned to Norway more determined than ever to make his work for Olympic Aid count. But he would need money...and lots of it.

Raising Money for Olympic Aid

When the 1994 Winter Olympics in Lillehammer were finally underway, Johann's focus shifted to becoming the best speed skater the world had ever seen. And yet, he hadn't forgotten all that he'd seen during his visit to Eritrea. For the time being, he tucked his

Credit: Right To Play

Years after giving away that first soccer ball, Johann still wants to see children everywhere having the opportunity to play.

memories of each of the children he'd met safely into the back of his mind and focused on the job of winning medals.

Johann skated better than ever before and won three gold medals. His first gold was for winning the 1500m race. Then he surprised the world by donating his $30,000 prize money to Olympic Aid. That wasn't all—Johann then challenged his fellow athletes and the public to a different kind of competition—one that raised $18 million for Olympic Aid! The money Johann and the other athletes raised that first winter went toward building a hospital in Sarajevo; helping a mother/infant program in Guatemala; caring for refugees in Afghanistan; supporting a program in

Lebanon for children with disabilities; and funding schools in Eritrea. What about the sports equipment he'd promised those boys?

Returning to Eritrea

One spring day, not long after the Winter Olympics were over, Johann was back in the air, flying to Eritrea for the second time. The plane was loaded with a variety of balls, track equipment, nets and goals, and other sports equipment. Johann was so excited he couldn't stop smiling. He felt like a skinny Norwegian version of Santa Claus bringing lots of gifts for deserving girls and boys. But when Johann picked up the Norwegian newspaper lying on the seat next to him, his mood quickly changed. One moment he'd been grinning ear to ear, and the next, the smile had melted from his face faster than snow in the hot African sun.

The newspaper report described the mass food shortages and starvation in Eritrea. The report also jeered at the young Olympic Aid member for being so clueless about the real needs of the people. What would starving children do with sports equipment, they asked? Johann spent the rest of the flight with an uneasy feeling at the bottom of his stomach. He dreaded having to meet with Eritrea's head of state, President Isaias Afewerki.

Amidst the cheers from the crowd who had gathered outside of the presidential palace, the two men reached out their hands to one another. Then Johann blurted, "I brought the wrong things, didn't I?"

As Johann recalls, President Isaias smiled and gestured to the crowd behind him. "They are here because of you, Mr. Koss. The equipment you bring from Norway's children is the first time we have felt like human beings. You see us as more than just bodies to be kept alive or mouths to feed. It symbolizes there is a hope for a peaceful future, and this is the first time my country's children will be able to play and to develop properly."

Later that year, Johann was presented with the 1994 Sportsman of the Year Award, along with many more prestigious awards. He was also appointed Special Representative for Sport for **UNICEF International.** Johann was only 26 years old when he retired from sports. He continued working for Olympic Aid, and soon led the organization in a new direction. Under Johann's guidance, it would become one of the most innovative and important charitable organizations in the world.

Right To Play

While the 1994 Winter Olympics faded into the past, Olympic Aid continued its work as the charitable arm of the Olympic Games for another six years. It partnered with other organizations, like UNICEF and the **World Health Organization (WHO)**, to bring aid to hundreds of thousands of people around the world. Olympic Aid helped raise millions of

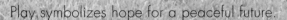

Play symbolizes hope for a peaceful future.

Credit: Istock

dollars, and the money was used to vaccinate over twelve million children and one million women. But even more astonishing was that this aid resulted in a truce between Afghanistan and the Kurdish region in northern Iraq. All fighting came to a stop for several days so UNICEF workers could safely administer the vaccinations.

By the late 1990s, it was clear that Olympic Aid's earlier goal of simply being a fundraising organization had changed. Johann and the other team members wanted to see it become a full-fledged non-government organization that would develop and implement its own programs around the world. They would need a new name, one that would clearly state what the team members had come to realize—that every child has the right to play. So, in 2000, the organization took on its new name—Right To Play—a title that affirms how essential sports and play are for every child's healthy development.

Johann continued working hard as Right To Play's president and chief executive officer. As a non-profit organization no longer attached to the Olympic Games, Right To Play was able to reach out to both Olympic athletes and other elite sports figures to become **Athlete Ambassadors**. It could now gain support in the private business world and from non-Olympic sports and athletes. Moreover, it had the freedom to become more involved at the grassroots level, to have an influence on government and UN policies involving children, and to begin conducting valuable research.

In early 2001, Right To Play's first sport and play programs were started in refugee camps in Angola and Cote d'Ivoire. Very quickly, its efforts spread across Africa, the Middle East, Asia and South America. Now, more than a decade after its birth, Right To Play provides programs and support in almost two dozen countries around the world.

"Look After Yourself, Look After One Another." This motto is written on every Right To Play soccer ball. This symbolic red ball is Right To Play's gift to every school, community and refugee camp that members visit. Coaches use it as their main teaching tool when emphasizing key points about fair play, peace, teamwork, respect, inclusion and healthy living. By the end of 2011, these ideals had reached nearly 835,000 children through weekly sport and play activities.

Historically, the Winter and Summer Olympic Games were held during the same year, but that all changed after 1992. Athletes like Johann Olav Koss, who had competed in the 1992 Winter Games, had the rare opportunity of competing just two years later when the Winter Olympics began its new four-year cycle in 1994.

Credit: istock.

"Going through refugee camps I realized the children weren't playing...they were [being] exposed to violence, sexual abuse, lack of education, and a total lack of hope that they might have a happy future. In the past, aid has been about food, shelter, water—but it is evolving to look at people as people... particularly children...and respecting all their needs. Here in Canada we take play for granted...but play is not a luxury. It has the potential to normalize a situation, to educate, and to help children going through trauma. Our red Right To Play ball not only provides children with the opportunity to play, it is a symbol for them to believe in the future, and it tells our philosophy. We see children learning to do that."

Johann Olav Koss

Credit: Nancy Zorzi

Girls from Pakistan play with the Right To Play red ball and know what it means to "Look After Yourself, Look After One Another."

John's Story: An Unexpected Turn of Events

Word spread quickly that a game of football was about to start in the field at the far end of the refugee camp. John Nsabimana dropped the heavy black pot he was scrubbing and shouted to his two younger brothers.

"Joseph! Samuel! Come on! They're starting a game!"*

The three boys weaved their way along the dusty and crowded passages of the Kigali refugee camp, dodging piles of garbage and debris, and passing men arguing and swearing at one another and a mother crying over the sick baby in her arms. Like most of the refugee children, John welcomed any distraction from the drudgery of his day-to-day life in the camp.

John was only thirteen and found it hard being the head of the family, always having to

be the responsible one. There was a time when he and his brothers lived a happy life with their parents in Rwanda. But those carefree days ended long ago in 1994, when months of chaos and ethnic killing tore his country and family to pieces. By the end of the bloodshed, his parents and most of his relatives had been killed. John and his brothers were among hundreds of thousands of children who were left orphaned by the genocide. With hardly any time to grieve, John and his brothers were swept up with millions of other survivors who fled across Rwanda's borders. The boys ended up in Uganda's largest refugee camp. Even though six years had passed since then, John had to try his best to forget those early days and focus on the present.

In a crowded refugee camp like this one

*At John's request, his brothers' names have been changed to protect their identities.

Credit: Istock

Children can make soccer balls out of almost anything laying around the house, including plastic bags and scraps of string.

in Kigali, there are few distractions, much violence, and even more hopeless despair. The children who grow up there have a hard time believing their futures will be any different. At the time, it certainly didn't look as if things would ever improve for John and his brothers either.

When the boys arrived at the field, the soccer game was well underway with plenty of spectators standing on the sidelines. The Nsabimana brothers watched and cheered as the barefooted players passed and kicked the homemade ball made of banana fibres tied with scraps of string. The game ended suddenly—as it usually did—when the feeble ball finally split into pieces. The crowd let out a loud groan and everyone slowly trickled back to their shacks and the usual grind of the day.

One day, not long after, there was a buzz in the camp. John heard the excited voices of children passing by on their way to the field. He quickly followed. What he saw when he arrived fascinated him—three strangers with yellow hair holding up shiny red soccer balls. The strangers announced to the children that they were volunteers from Right To Play Canada and had come to teach them some games from their **Live Safe, Play Safe** program. None of the children had ever heard of Right To Play before, but no one could resist the chance to play with the colourful new soccer balls.

Neither John nor any of the other children realized how the course of their lives had suddenly changed that day—all because of a game. Not only did Right To Play introduce them to a life that included sports and play, but those young Canadian volunteers soon became like family to the orphaned children. As the weeks and months passed by, the

Today, in Kigali, Rwanda, children are again finding joy in a simple ball game.

Credit: Right To Play

Credit: Tara Morris

The Live Safe, Play Safe program is all fun and games—but it's also how Right To Play volunteers teach kids to make good choices that will keep them safe and healthy.

children of the Kigali refugee camp learned how to protect themselves from disease, how to resolve conflicts with others, and how to laugh again.

Amazingly, with help from the Right To Play mentors, John was given the opportunity to attend high school—something he never dreamed would be possible. In time, he found a way to give back—he became an enthusiastic Right To Play volunteer and coached hundreds of the Kigali refugee children how to use sports and play to improve their lives too.

Then one day, he was flying off to the icy cold climate of eastern Canada to begin his studies at Pearson College.

Today, John is an earnest young man, learning how to improve the lives of others. He is earning a degree at the University of Victoria and is interested in social development and child-protection issues. He is now a spokesman for Right To Play and the Regional Youth Representative for UNICEF British Columbia.

"I was lucky. I don't think I had anything special about me, but for some reason I was picked. Maybe it was because of my sense of responsibility for the other kids," he reflects quietly. "One day I want to go back and help Rwanda. I want to start a program that will benefit my people the way that Right To Play has helped me and so many others."

Here's a Game to Try: Homemade Balls

What you'll need:

- Old socks, nylons, rags, a long-sleeved shirt, newspaper, or a balloon
- String, wool or tape

Instructions:

1. Search around the house for things you might be able to use to create a ball.
2. Try making a few balls using different methods and materials and then test them out.
3. Take your best ball to school and organize a game of soccer or catch.

Results:

How long did your ball last? How easy was it to use? How does it compare to the professionally made balls you're used to? How could you modify your ball for someone who was blind? (How about putting a little bell inside the ball when you are making it?)

Credit: Anto1210

"...We are all equally responsible for the lives of these children; they are all our children. Government and non-governmental organizations need to work towards creating a brighter and safer world for children that live in unsafe circumstances."

Haile Gebrselassie, Athlete Ambassador and Olympic gold medalist from Ethiopia (long-distance track)

Credit: Right To Play

Children in Jericho learn about teamwork and cooperation on a Play Day.

Chapter 3

The Right To Play Team

Have you ever wondered what it takes to be a hero? Being some kind of a superhuman—possessing dazzling strength, speed and good looks wouldn't be a bad start. If you added a dose or two of crime-busting, puzzle-solving braininess, you would have a top-notch hero, right? Excluding action figures and comic-book characters of course—do you know anybody like that?

If you're interested in real heroes, Right To Play has tons. Some are well known, like hockey great Wayne Gretzky; and Olympic gold medalists Clara Hughes, Simon Whitfield and Haile Gebrselassie. Others are in-

fluential, like Her Royal Highness Princess Haya Bint Al Hussein. But most Right To Play heroes are regular people just like you. Have you ever heard of Yonas Tadesse or Mzaliwa Salima of Africa? They're volunteer Coaches for Right To Play. What about Tahmina Khan, an Afghani refugee in Pakistan or Bashira Edgheim of Lebanon? They're both teachers who use Right To Play programs in their schools under the most difficult circumstances. As for kid heroes—well, Right To Play has them too, like eleven-year-old Canadian Mohamad Assaf. The one thing these heroes all have in common is the realization that sports, play, and laughter are key ingredients for a happy childhood. They all want to help bring these elements into the lives of children around the world.

Athlete Ambassadors

Runners who have sprinted down a track at top speed have felt it. So have high divers springing into the cool water below with perfect form. And certainly, any soccer player who has kicked a ball into the net has also felt the absolute joy that comes from being active, doing his or her best, and being part of a team. The Olympic and professional athletes who are Athlete Ambassadors for Right To Play know from their experiences how important play and sports are for healthy development. With support from family, friends and communities, these athletes were able to rise to the top of their game. Now that they have won the

Credit: Right To Play

Girls and boys in Pakistan, playing games together.

respect and attention of the public, they are in the position to use their celebrity to give back. Today, there are hundreds of Olympic and professional athletes from dozens of

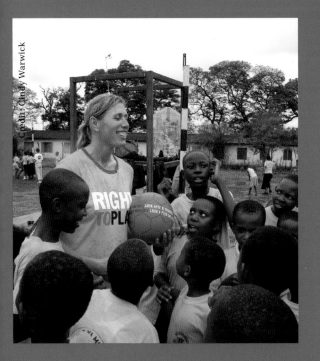

Credit: Cindy Warwick

"Sport has influenced the path my life has taken. It has given me the ability to focus, create vision, understand differences and persevere through adversity. Going into the field in Africa brought home the reality that many children do not have the opportunity to engage in sport or to play. I had believed that these benefits were available to every child. In the refugee camps in Sudan I saw children whose days were void of anything but intense boredom. To these children, Right To Play and our partners bring play, and with play the opportunity to learn and grow and develop their potential. Play is not a luxury; it is an essential element to a child's development."

Silken Laumann, Athlete Ambassador and three-time Olympic medalist (rowing)

Credit: Right To Play

Young men confined to refugee camps are often the worst hit by lack of opportunity. These young people at Umphium Refugee Camp in Thailand are learning that there is always a way to serve the community.

> "Sports can shape an individual's confidence, self-esteem, morals, strength, and physical and mental well being. With some children going through devastation in their lives, depriving them of the right to play could deprive them of a chance to truly live a fulfilled life. Thinking of the smile that I can help put on the face of a small child makes every effort worthwhile."
>
> *Nikki Stone, Athlete Ambassador and Olympic gold medalist (aerials)*

countries giving time and energy to serve as Athlete Ambassadors; in Canada, there are over 120 Ambassadors on the Right To Play team.

One way Athlete Ambassadors help is by raising awareness about those children whose lives are plagued by extreme poverty, disease, war, and other calamities. While these children are desperate for food, clothing and stability, they are also in need of hope and joy—and that is something that play and sports can give them. Athlete Ambassadors use their influence to educate the public, as well as world leaders, business people, and other decision makers who can donate money for Right To Play programming. Athlete Ambassadors help in other ways too. They attend community events and give talks on the importance of play for healthy development. They often donate their own money and let their names and faces be used for promotion. Many travel to developing countries like Rwanda, Liberia, Benin, Ghana and Mali to introduce sports and play to desperate communities where former child soldiers, victims of war, and refugees far from home are living. Athlete Ambassadors also campaign for fundraisers, donate their equipment for online auctions, and encourage other star athletes to become Athlete Ambassadors too.

Athlete Ambassadors promote and teach

skills like dedication, leadership and respect. So they need to be excellent role models and demonstrate these qualities—not only out on the track, field or slopes, but in their everyday lives too. As role models, they inspire children to take part in solving the world's problems and raising awareness and funds for Right To Play programs. The work Athlete Ambassadors do provides them with a genuine opportunity to change the world for the better.

A New Challenge

Nakivale refugee camp in Uganda is home to almost 50,000 refugees. These children and adults were forced to flee from their homes just to stay alive. They face immense poverty and rampant disease, and live with unspoken heartache and conflict. Here is what Athlete Ambassador and Olympic rower, Jane Rumball, wrote after visiting the camp in 2009:

"Before we got to Uganda, it was sometimes hard to imagine what I could offer. I have

Credit: Istock

Athlete Ambassadors raise awareness about the lives of the most disadvantaged children all over the world.

Right To Play Athlete Ambassador, Jane Rumball, plays a circle game with children in Uganda.

Credit: Right To Play

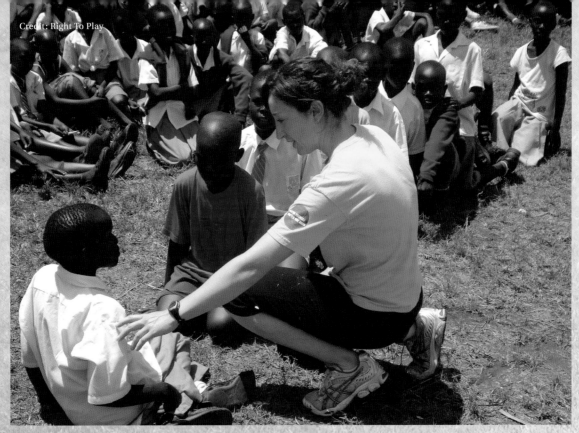

Credit: Right To Play

Athlete Ambassador, Jane Rumball, teaches these Ugandan children about rowing.

lived my life in relative luxury and comfort, participating in a sport that is only accessible to the wealthy. The Ugandan Right To Play staff explained the value of the role, though, and it made it crystal clear. The children look forward to the Athlete Ambassadors' visits with huge expectation. A *muzungu*, a white person, and one who went to the Olympics, actually cares enough to visit them. They know that our presence means that they are not forgotten, that we are trying to do our part to help them and we know their cause.

I tried to take on this challenge and participate with my whole being. This meant fully participating in the games, taking time to talk to as many children as possible, and saying a few words to the children. I tried my best to teach them how to row! One of the times,

our coxswain (the smallest volunteer in the group) fell over laughing at the absurdity of it all. It made me wonder if our own coxswain (Olympic gold medalist Lesley Thompson-Willie) actually felt that way sometimes too!

"At a particularly difficult stop along the way in Nakivale, I found a little friend who I will never forget. She was a beautiful but severely malnourished girl who held tightly onto my hand throughout all the games. She had severely infected bumps on the side of her head, but still tried to dress up with earrings that looked like they were fashioned out of paper clips. Once she realized that she could hold my hand, she started to rub her face on my arm. For a brief moment I wanted to pull away for fear of somehow getting that infection transmitted to my own skin...but

Credit: Right To Play

These Coaches from Ghana show the children how simple it is to get a polio vaccination.

then I realized that most people probably do draw back and make her feel bad. I wanted to be different and let her just stay put beside me for the rest of the session. It ended up being a very special moment for both of us, I think. She started to get into the games and laughed and danced like the other children around her."

Volunteer Coaches

If Right To Play was a sports car—let's say a bright red Ferrari--then the Athlete Ambassador would be the cool exterior and shiny chrome, while the local volunteer Coach would be the powerful engine. These Coaches are what take that Ferrari streaking down the highway.

A Coach is sometimes someone who has already been nurturing young people in a community—such as a teacher or village elder. But lately, many of the local volunteer Coaches are men and women who once participated in Right To Play's sports and play programs as children. As kids, they looked forward to learning new games each week, meeting children from neighbouring communities during **Play Days,** feeling the support of nurturing adults, and being part of a team. While they were playing, having fun, learning new skills, and gaining confidence in themselves, they were also developing the perfect qualities of a volunteer Coach—compassion, selfless commitment, and a desire to make their small part of the world a better place. Before becoming a Coach for Right To Play, all volunteers undergo training, which helps them deliver the programs more effectively.

Children whose lives are embedded in

Credit: United States Marine Corps

Volunteer Coaches are often nurturing adults, like village elders.

Every child is potentially the community's next leader and volunteer Coach.

There are more than 15,000 Right To Play volunteer Coaches in more than 20 countries around the world, including Indonesia, Jordan, Lebanon, Liberia, Mali, Pakistan, Peru, Palestinian Territories, Rwanda, Thailand, and Uganda.

Given that Right To Play is a humanitarian organization with lots of Olympic athlete volunteers, you might naturally assume their volunteer Coaches would all be the fastest, fittest and strongest examples of the perfect athletes too. But a person doesn't need to be a great athlete in order to be a great volunteer Coach.

poverty, disease, war or any other kind of tragedy benefit tremendously from having a volunteer Coach. These Coaches bring out the children's creativity, talents, confidence, and enthusiasm through games, sports and discussions. They also model respect, teamwork, cooperation and communication for the children—skills they will need to improve the quality of their lives. Often the relationships formed between these mentors and children are long term and help kids cope with all the challenges life throws their way. Regular participation in sports and play programs also helps to provide a sense of normalcy—even under the worst circumstances.

Volunteer Coaches have a great opportunity to shape children's attitudes by presenting concepts that are progressive and positive, and that foster a desire to become good citizens.

Giving Back

When Christopher Zigbu was a child refugee in Guinea, he had the opportunity to participate in a Right To Play program. Then the fighting stopped in Liberia and he was able to return home where he planned to go back to school and become a doctor. But after seeing how desperate the children were for activity and fitness at the refugee camp, he decided he had to do something to help the children in his homeland too. So he became a volunteer Coach and started his own Right To Play program.

"I started a sports and play program for the local school children in Liberia. At first, the school wanted to pay me for my work. But just as others have given to me in a time of need, it was only right that I give back. So instead of accepting pay, I used the money to buy equipment for the children."

Christopher Zigbu, Right To Play volunteer Coach, Monrovia, Liberia

Children whose lives are disrupted by tragedy benefit enormously from having volunteer Coaches in their community.

Yonas's Story: I Can Do It

It was the first day and Yonas Tadesse was nervous. Not as many children had shown up to his new Right To Play sport and play program as he had hoped. But then, he had to be honest with himself. He knew the day he posted the notice on the school bulletin board that it was going to be tough getting parents, teachers, and children to accept him in his new role. He shifted uncomfortably on his crutches and hoped his shaky legs, crippled by polio, would hold him now, when he needed them most. For a brief moment, Yonas looked down at himself and wondered: What was I thinking when I agreed to become a sports coach for children?

But then, like a supersonic eraser wiping chalk off a blackboard, he erased that self-condemning thought. Instead, he remembered the promise he made to himself only months before. "I will never look to the past again."

If there was anyone who had a reason to feel sorry about his past, it was Yonas. When he was a young boy, his homeland, Ethiopia, was suffering under cruel leadership. Many of the ethnic groups were fighting each other, AIDS was killing thousands, and millions more were starving because of a food shortage caused by a terrible drought. In Yonas's case, there were even more difficulties. Within a very short time, both of his parents died, and he became crippled by polio—all before he was even ten years old.

Being an orphan as well as having a

disability was hard. Yonas felt that others merely saw him as the boy who was crippled, weak, and different; not as the boy with a big heart, the boy who was good with numbers, or the boy who had a bright smile. As time went by, he stopped playing, shied away from other children, and finally quit school.

For Yonas, the worst part of school was always physical education class. It was the time when everyone focused on his disability. He felt like an alien from some faraway planet. If that wasn't hard enough, his teachers worried that he might get hurt so they discouraged him from participating.

"Sit on the sideline and watch, Yonas; it will be safer for you there." Those words stung as he watched the other children laughing and running around. Would he really never know the joy of sports and play?

For a couple of years after quitting school, Yonas watched from life's sideline, tried to be invisible, and thought only of the things he would never do. He was discouraged, alone and alienated; his life felt like a moonless night. But then something happened—something that, at the time, seemed hardly worth noting—something that would soon turn his dark nights into bright, sunny days and change the way he thought about himself and others.

"Yonas, there are some people here in Kirkos who are looking for volunteer Coaches to work with the children after school," said one of the elders. At first, Yonas thought the man was making a cruel joke. "These people call their organization Right To Play and they're looking for someone just like you." Yonas looked down at himself and wondered how it was possible. Did they know about all the things he could not do?

Credit: Right To Play

The five coloured rings that form the symbol for the Olympics are also used to symbolize the different kinds of Right To Play games.

Yonas soon found out that the organizers from Right To Play were not concerned about what he *could not* do but were interested in all the things he *could* do. They wanted to see him become a role model for youth. They were looking for someone who would help children develop life skills no matter what their physical ability.

Now, as Yonas stood before the children on the starting day of his Right To Play sports and play program, it felt like a million years ago that he lacked self-confidence, ambition or zest for life. It felt like a million years ago that he was just the boy with a disability. He held up a shiny red ball and asked the children, "Who can tell me what this says?"

Volunteer Coach, Yonas Tadesse, is one of Right To Play's everyday heroes.

One boy's arm shot up. "I can read," he blurted. Yonas smiled and invited him to take the ball and read the words out loud to the other children. "It says, 'Look After Yourself, Look After One Another.'"

"That's right, and that's just what we're going to do...we're going to learn, through games and play, how to take care of ourselves and one another. We're going to find out that everyone is good at something and that no matter what our physical challenges, we all have the right to play."

When Yonas first started as a volunteer Coach, he got little support from the community, but today, nearly a hundred children

come three times a week to participate in his play program. Parents also seek him out for help with their children, and elders and other youth organizations invite him to give inspirational talks. Right To Play organizers have even given him the responsibility of training new Coaches.

"I used to focus on what I couldn't do, but I no longer worry about those things. Instead, I face my challenges, and say, 'Why not? I can do it.'"

~

In 2007, the United Nations and the Ethiopian Federation for People Living with Disabilities gave Right To Play an award for being the

Credit: Right To Play

Credit: Nancy Zorzi

Left: Emmanuel Ofosu Yeboah advocates for respect and acceptance in Ghana. Right: Boys in Pakistan create new games with their shiny red ball.

best international NGO (non-governmental organization) helping people with disabilities. In Ethiopia, there are 4.5 million people with disabilities caused by things like landmines and polio. Before Right To Play's programs, children with disabilities rarely got the chance to attend school or participate in sports and play. Now, many of these youths have become Coaches and role models for other children with disabilities.

Right To Play has many other team members behind the scenes too, like the athlete supporters. These men and women are local sports figures in places like North America or Europe, who help raise awareness in their communities about Right To Play and the importance of sports and play for children in developing countries. They attend events and generate interest within the sporting communities and among fellow athletes—all in an effort to raise funds for sports and play programs. Some Right To Play team members work in international offices. Others are organizers who work in the field, meeting with community leaders in order to set up programs, find potential volunteer Coaches and provide training. Ultimately, every project's goal is to create a strong program that is eventually self-sustaining and completely run by local members of the communities who benefit from the Right To Play programs.

Here's a Game to Try: Tunnel Ball

What you'll need:

- At least six friends
- A ball

Instructions:

1. Players form a circle, standing with legs apart.
2. The player who is IT stands in the middle with the ball and tries to roll it between the legs of one of the other players. The players can try to prevent the ball from going between their legs using their hands to stop it, but they must not move their feet.
3. When the ball rolls between a player's legs, then that player goes into the middle of the circle with the ball and becomes IT and the former middle player joins the circle.

Results:

Yonas wants to see all children be able to participate in games. Can you think of some ways this game could be modified to include children with various disabilities? How would a game like this build a child's self-esteem and confidence? It's easy to learn and easy to play.

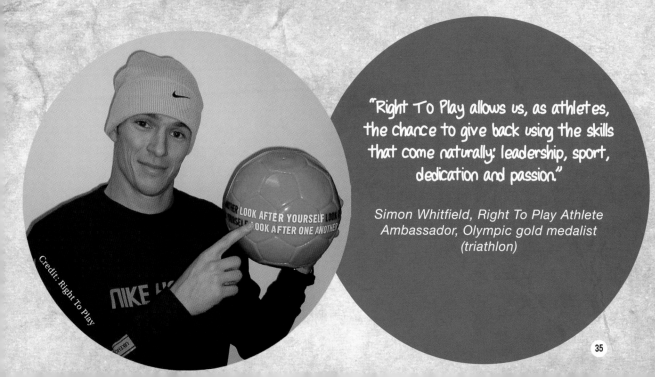

Credit: Right To Play

"Right To Play allows us, as athletes, the chance to give back using the skills that come naturally: leadership, sport, dedication and passion."

Simon Whitfield, Right To Play Athlete Ambassador, Olympic gold medalist (triathlon)

35

Credit: Right To Play

At a Play Day in Thailand, these children are wearing shirts and holding posters featuring the five colours of Right to Play.

Chapter 4

Playing the Game

You probably don't need an Olympic or professional athlete to convince you that play and sports are important elements in a kid's life. Still, it's nice to know grown-ups agree that when you're busy playing street hockey or chasing after a soccer ball, you're doing important stuff.

Sadly, millions of children haven't experienced this right to play. That's why it's Right To Play's mission to ensure that all children receive the opportunities to grow up healthy and peacefully, and to experience joy and laughter through sports and play. First and foremost, the programs offered are *fun*! But underneath that fun are lessons—lessons about fair play, teamwork, respect, commitment, conflict resolution and health. Some games have additional purposes, like giving kids the tools to say no to peer pressure and to overcome barriers based on gender or physical ability. None of this would be possible if it weren't for the caring volunteers who nurture, guide and teach the children.

Game Rules

While fun is important, there are two key underlying purposes for Right To Play's sports and play programs: one is to teach children how to live healthy lives and the other is to help them become productive members of society. **SportWork** programs use sports and play to develop children's physical, social and emotional well being. They provide opportunities for kids to practise life skills, such as cooperation, leadership and persistence. **SportHealth** programs, on the other hand, focus on teaching children about health issues. These events may involve educational games on HIV/AIDS or malaria protection. Sometimes, SportHealth events are also opportunities to immunize children against specific diseases.

SportWork and SportHealth programs sometimes bring together several communities and take the form of large sports meets. Other times, the programs are just meant for local children. Either way, the volunteer Coaches and community leaders ensure the games and activities incorporate local cultures and education systems.

Credit: Right To Play

With Right To Play's history strongly connected to the Olympics, it's natural that the organization has incorporated many Olympic ideals and symbols into its programs. The widely known five-coloured rings that symbolize the Olympics have come to represent the five areas of development that Right To Play games address.

- **Red Mind Ball** games: develop concentration, perception, problem-solving skills and creativity.
- **Black Body Ball** games: focus on physical development—skill, endurance and flexibility, and establishing an ongoing love for sports and play.
- **Yellow Spirit Ball** games: build on emotional development, such as self-esteem, acceptance, social skills, and confidence.
- **Blue Peace Ball** games: center on developing relationships, resolving conflicts and working through feelings of fear.
- **Green Health Ball** games: teach children ways of staying healthy, like regularly washing hands, using mosquito nets and avoiding sexually transmitted diseases.

Credit: Right To Play

"I want everyone to understand the urgency and importance of Right To Play's mission: to create a healthier and safer world for children through the power of sport and play. This is far more important than any gold medals, even an Olympic gold medal."

Clara Hughes, Athlete Ambassador, Summer and Winter Olympic medalist (cycling and speed skating)

Credit: Right To Play

In Tamani, Mali community members participate in a Right To Play Live Safe, Play Safe game.

Obstacles to Play

Despite Right To Play's best intentions, there have been many roadblocks to overcome in the effort to bring sports and play into the lives of children in need. Obtaining the money needed to provide equipment, training and facilities is a big concern. And some people still think that play and sports are not important in the lives of children.

Sometimes, Right To Play organizers have to figure out how to introduce programs when there are cultural barriers. For some local people, the idea of volunteering is new. These are people who must work long, hard hours just to earn enough money to feed their families. Often, before Right To Play organizers can recruit potential volunteer

Credit: Right To Play China

Understanding other cultures helps Right To Play volunteers promote sports and play.

Coaches, they must first convince community leaders of the programs' benefits. They help them see that giving away time and energy, in order for children to have sports and play, is worthwhile; that physical activity helps

Credit: Right To Play

Most kids would rather go for a hot dog at half-time, but at this Right To Play football match in Mali they get vaccination shots.

to reduce depression, physical illness and weakness, while increasing academic success and earning potential for boys and girls alike.

In some cases, prejudice presents a barrier to providing sports and play to children. These exclusions are sometimes racial, but they are also often caused by cultural attitudes toward girls or children with disabilities. In some societies there are **gender rules**—expected behaviours and activities that are specific to males and females. In many cultures, girls are expected to live by different standards than boys. They often have fewer rights and more responsibilities at a very young age. As a result, they have less opportunity to participate in sports and play, and often suffer from poor mental, emotional, and physical health. Even the clothing girls must wear in some cultures can present an obstacle to running and playing freely.

Right To Play often works in communities where gender-related limits are prevalent. In some cases, organizers have introduced play opportunities that are specifically designed for girls. These "girls only" games and sports events accommodate local cultural norms that do not permit girls and boys to play together and require girls to wear bulky clothing that covers their entire bodies.

In the following story you'll learn how one girl's life and ideals changed when Right To Play came to town.

Credit: Right To Play

These Thai boys and girls participated in the World Aids Day festivities.

Esther's Story: Having a Dream

It was a Tuesday morning and the children were filing into the one-room school in Teboman Quarter. Esther sat near the back with the older children, while the teacher stood at the front and waited for everyone's attention.

"I have an announcement to make," she told the children. "There is to be an exciting event sponsored by a humanitarian organization called Right To Play. The members of this organization believe it's important for all children to play. They are going to train Coaches here in Lofa County who will prepare you for a great football tournament that will take place on International Peace Day."

At first, only the boys began to chatter excitedly about the wonderful event. Then the teacher continued.

"This football tournament is not only for the boys," she said. "Every team must have an equal amount of girl players too."

"We'll never win if we have to play with girls on our team," groaned some of the boys. In fact, the boys were not the only ones who objected to girls playing football. Parents, villagers, and even some of the girls themselves didn't see why Right To Play insisted they participate in the tournament. But not Esther; when she heard the news, she began to tingle from head to toe. You see, Esther grew up being taught that girls are not as good as boys, but in her heart, she never believed it was true.

For most of her life, Esther's little country of Liberia, in West Africa, was in a state of civil war. The war ended in 2003, but the country was still badly broken down from fifteen years of fighting among rival tribes. During that time, homes and buildings were flattened, roads were destroyed, and communication systems were wiped out. Hateful things were said and done, and it took a long time for wounds to begin healing.

After the war ended, Esther was happy she could finally go to school. But during lunchtime and after school, she often longed to be out on the dusty playground with the boys, chasing after one of their crazy, lopsided homemade balls. Girls were never encouraged or invited to play. Most spent their after-school hours doing chores or looking after their younger siblings. They were destined to become young wives and mothers who would soon have no need or time for play and sports.

When the Right To Play volunteers arrived, they brought brand new, shiny red soccer balls. Esther liked the words written on the balls: "Look After Yourself, Look After One Another." She decided it was a good motto to try to live her life by. The volunteer Coaches taught the boys and girls games and football

Credit: Andrew Moir

In many countries, young girls are often responsible for maintaining the household and looking after younger children. They have little time to play.

These Ethiopian children find joy and freedom during a Play Day.

Credit: Right To Play

Credit: Right To Play China

These Chinese girls play a game of Frozen Beanbag.

drills. The children also learned what it truly meant to be peaceful, cooperative, encouraging, and inclusive of everyone—regardless of skill, ability or gender. Soon, even the parents began to notice how well the children were getting along, and how much happier and energetic they all seemed to be.

Whenever Esther could, she'd encourage her teammates by saying things like, "good try," "nice shot," or "you'll get it next time." Everyone noticed her enthusiasm and sportsmanship—even the boys. Imagine how she felt the day her teammates chose her to become their team captain.

"Being captain of the Voinjama Young Starts is a job I will take seriously," she promised. Esther's smile reached from ear to ear.

For weeks, Esther and the volunteer Coaches worked hard to improve everyone's skills. As the day of the great tournament approached, the students decorated banners with sayings like, "Every Child Has the Right To Play" and "When Children Play, The World Wins!" Incredibly, busloads of students from Vahun District, Logan Town and other small villages came to join the celebration. There they all were—boys and girls whose families were once enemies during Liberia's civil war—playing and laughing and treating each other with support and respect. Not a trace of the old resentment was to be found anywhere that day.

At the end of the tournament, Esther happily waved goodbye to her new friends and all the visiting teams. She couldn't help smiling. Not so long ago, the idea of a peaceful Liberia where boys and girls could play together on a football field—and even those from opposing tribes—seemed to be a distant dream. Now anything was possible—and Esther could have dreams of her own.

Not long after, the lanky teenage girl made an announcement to her friends and family.

"I have decided it will be my lifelong quest to become the president of Liberia," she stated. Her eyes sparkled and she was smiling, and in that moment, nobody laughed or doubted the sincerity of her words.

Here's a Game to Try: Frozen Beanbag

What you'll need:

- At least six players
- One beanbag for each player (if beanbags are not available, try filling old socks with pea gravel and tying them off at the top with string)

Instructions:

1. Decide the boundaries of the play area.
2. Give each player a beanbag to balance on his or her head.
3. Players move around the play area fast or slow. If a player's beanbag falls off, then she is frozen.
4. Another player can retrieve the fallen beanbag and place it back on the frozen player's head. But it must be done without that player losing her own beanbag.
5. The game can be made more challenging by moving faster, creating obstacles or having more than one beanbag per player.

Results:

This is a good game for teaching empathy, cooperation and respect. Did you see players who were willing to risk losing their own beanbags to help someone else? Remember the Right To Play motto? "Look After Yourself, Look After One Another."

Credit: Right To Play

HRH Princess Haya Bint Al Hussein, Athlete Ambassador (Wife to HH Sheikh Mohammed Bin Rashid Al Maktoum, Vice President and Prime Minister of the UAE, Ruler of Dubai, daughter to King Hussein of Jordan)

"Sport has a natural and universal power to attract, inspire, motivate and engage. Sport is everywhere. And everywhere that it is, sport demonstrates its capacity to move people emotionally and physically. Right To Play's programs were developed around the simple premise that we could translate this love of sport into an opportunity to promote health and well being throughout the world."

Credit: Right To Play

Everyone here took the Right To Play pledge!

Chapter 5

A Team Anyone Can Join

Think about any team that you (or your friends) have been a part of and recall the commitment that was required. Before the games even started you probably dedicated several hours to getting in shape and practising, and perhaps even raising funds for team uniforms. Maybe you volunteered to keep the equipment and the field in good condition during the season. And so, like any other team you've been a part of, there is also a commitment if you want to join Right To Play: *Look After Yourself, Look After One Another*—that is the Right To Play philosophy.

So how does someone like you fulfill the requirements of that idea? One thing you can do is start talking to people about the importance of sports and play in kids' lives. You've been reading about how playing builds self-esteem, improves health, educates children and brings joy and happiness—especially to the world's most disadvantaged children. So start by telling your family and friends about these benefits, then branch out to your neighbourhood and school community. Introduce them to Right To Play and explain how it has been helping to improve the lives of children who live with poverty, disease and war by providing them with opportunities to play, learn and be healthy.

One more thing—don't forget the first part

of the philosophy! Make sure you are looking after yourself by making time for active play and sports that leave you feeling happy and healthy. Then read on to learn about the ways that other people—kids included—are volunteering to help the world's disadvantaged children participate in play and sports.

Why Be a Volunteer?

Volunteering means working without pay or benefit to oneself. Yet when people volunteer, they can't help but benefit themselves. There are lots of advantages in volunteering. For starters, it's a way to make new friends—possibly friends from all over the world! It's a great way to learn things and develop interests; it gives a sense of satisfaction; and it can be fun and energizing. It's also a way to complete the picture of who you really are—by demonstrating your interests, passion, dedication and caring commitment to others.

Volunteerism is so important to United States President Barack Obama that he initiated a program called **United We Serve.** He believes—and so do many others—that volunteering is important to the success of a society and should be a way of life for everyone. It's how ordinary people band together to achieve extraordinary things. It's a commitment by kids, teens and adults to give back to society—whether locally, nationally or internationally.

Right To Play is a member of United We Serve. So when people like you volunteer to raise awareness and funds so children in need can have the right to play, you're also taking part in a worldwide movement that is encouraging others to volunteer too. Don't let anyone tell you that because you're a kid, you're too small to make a difference in the world. Anyone who has ever spent the night with a mosquito buzzing around the room will tell you it's not size that counts, but determination and persistence!

It was a sweltering hot day—not at all unusual

Credit: United States Senate

"I'm not telling you what your role should be, that's for you to discover. But I am asking you to stand up and play your part!"

US President Barack Obama, on United We Serve Volunteerism

Credit: Kate Duhamel

Because of the efforts of volunteers and fundraisers, programs like this one in Lebanon are available to children around the world.

Mohamad's Story: Making a Difference

for Toronto in July. What made it bearable for one seven-year-old boy was the anticipation of watching the final match between Italy and France in the 2006 World Cup.

Mohamad Assaf prided himself on knowing his soccer statistics and was betting on Italy taking the cup for the fourth time. He couldn't have been more excited if it were his own soccer team about to play in the big event. As he sat watching the pre-game banter and entertainment, he realized he was thirsty.

"Okay folks, we'll be back for the start of the game just after this commercial break," said the announcer.

Great, Mohamad thought. He grabbed his empty glass and darted for the kitchen, but suddenly stopped at the sight of a sad-looking African boy on the TV. The ad talked about how, in some countries, children had to fight

as soldiers, were poor, sick or orphaned. "But every child should have the ordinary right to play," the voice declared. Then a bold red soccer ball and banner that read "Support Children's Right To Play" filled the screen.

As he wandered into the kitchen, Mohamad thought about how much he loved playing sports. He had a hard time imagining how there could be kids in the world who would never have the same opportunity to play as he did. He thought it was unfair. But he just shrugged his shoulders while the voice inside his head told him there was nothing he could do about it. After all, *I'm just a kid*, he thought.

Two years later, as Mohamad recalls, his grade 4 teacher, Mr. Galvin, made an announcement to the class.

"It's important for you to know how fortunate you are compared to many people in the world. Your assignment is to find a charitable organization and learn how it's helping people in need." Then Mr. Galvin pointed at everyone and said, "It's also possible for boys and girls like you to make a difference in the world. So come up with some ideas about how you can help other people."

That night, Mohamad sat at the kitchen table looking over the list of charities on his homework sheet. He was excited about helping people in need, but he couldn't seem to decide which charity he should pick. They were all good!

Just then, his battered, old soccer ball sitting at the back door caught his attention. It tweaked his memory and he suddenly recalled the haunting face of the boy on the TV. What was the name of that charity? Bingo! He remembered—Right To Play!

The more he thought about it, the more he liked the idea. Mohamad loved sports and playing games with his friends, so Right To Play was the perfect charity. Even if it was a homework assignment, he liked the idea of helping other kids.

Mohamad thoroughly researched the Right To Play organization. He found out the head office was in Toronto, not far from where he lived, and that it had programs in Africa, Asia and soon, South America. He found a poster board and pasted on information and pictures of barefooted kids playing soccer in Uganda, others getting immunized in Sierra Leone, and Palestinian girls learning to play games in Ramallah. In big, bold letters was the Right To Play motto "Look After Yourself, Look After One Another." He also liked their other saying—"When Children Play, The World Wins!" So he used that one too.

On presentation day, Mohamad looked for-

Credit: Lisa Assaf

Mohamad Assaf told his friends and neighbours about Right To Play and raised money for their programs.

ward to telling the class about the charity he'd picked. He started by saying, "I love to play sports and love to help kids. So that's why I picked Right To Play for my project." He later taught his classmates some of the games Right To Play uses when teaching children about staying healthy, like Flu Tag. He also shared the Canadian school program called **Learning to Play, Playing to Learn**. His project got such a good response that it gave him confidence to talk about Right To Play to other people, like his friends, neighbours and even strangers passing by on the street. Then he got another idea—he would start raising money for Right To

"Never doubt that a small group of committed people can change the world. Indeed, it is the only thing that ever has."

Margaret Mead, anthropologist and author

Like Mohamad, these boys are passionate about playing soccer.

Credit: Right To Play

Play's projects! There was no better place to start than at his mosque.

"Did you know there are children in some parts of the world who never get the chance to play and have fun?" Mohamad asked a man who had stopped to admire his display. The grey-haired man shook his head. "But that's starting to change because of Right To Play and their Athlete Ambassadors and volunteer Coaches," he continued. After listening to what Mohamad had to say, the man donated five dollars. Soon, others were dropping money into his donation box too. By the time he left the mosque, Mohamad had raised $1,000 and educated many people about Right To Play's work.

He didn't stop there though; he got another big idea. He knew every kid in his school liked to play and figured they'd all like to have one of the mini Right To Play red soccer balls. He was right; he raised another $200 by selling them to kids in his school.

Mohamad continues to volunteer for Right To Play by educating people about the importance of play and sports. He still likes to tell people about Right To Play's work, and sells mini soccer balls and t-shirts. To date, he has raised over $2,000—enough money for twenty children to participate in Right To Play programs for a year.

"When you give back, it feels better than anything in the world," Mohamad said. "I like knowing that I've helped kids who might otherwise never get the chance to play games like soccer. It's just like they said: 'Look After Yourself, Look After One Another.'"

Here's a Game to Try: Volunteer Volleyball

What you'll need:

- Best with about ten players divided into two teams
- A volleyball
- If a volleyball net is available, use it

Instructions:

1. This game is played much like regular volleyball when it comes to serving, spiking and scoring points. One side serves the ball to the other. The other side hits the ball back without catching it. A point is scored if the ball falls to the ground within the boundaries.

2. Begin the game. After a player scores she must then run over to the other team and volunteer to help them.

3. Similarly, when the opposing team scores a point their player runs to the opposite team to volunteer.

4. If team sizes get lopsided, someone simply calls out "Do we have any volunteers?" At this time, any player can run across to the other side.

Results:

Can you tell which team is the winning team? One thing is for sure—there won't be any losers! This adaptation to the game of volleyball can be applied to all sorts of games, such as basketball or baseball. The main point is that the players move between teams as points are scored.

Credit: Right To Play

"This is one of the greatest causes I have ever seen. Right To Play is using the incredible power of sport and play to help children who are in refugee camps, affected by war, and orphaned by HIV/AIDS."

Wayne Gretzky, Right To Play Athlete Ambassador, Olympic gold medalist and hockey star

Credit: Right To Play

Credit: Gina McMurchy-B

Left: Children in Ramallah, Palestine, during a Play Day celebration. Right: The City of Surrey celebrates with Right To Play during the 2010 Winter Olympics in Vancouver, British Columbia.

Chapter 6

Becoming a Team Member

You now know how one person can make a big difference when it comes to helping children in need. So imagine what happens when a whole bunch of people get behind the same cause—mega-good stuff, for sure. The citizens of Surrey, British Columbia know because that's just what happened when the students, teachers, local government and businesses jumped at the opportunity to make Right To Play their charitable partner during the 2010 Winter Olympics.

"For Surrey, this partnership with Right To Play represents an opportunity to truly make a difference, embrace global citizenry, and focus on the most important asset of any city's future, our children," said Surrey's mayor, Dianne Watts.

City staff and Right To Play organizers worked out a plan that drew on the potential of every elementary and high-school student in the city. by sending Olympic Athlete Ambassadors to all the schools to get them excited about Right To Play. These Athlete Ambassadors encouraged students to commit to their own improved health and wellness through an active lifestyle, but also urged them to join the effort to raise funds that would give this same opportunity to disadvantaged children in other parts of the world. Many teachers

50

and students eagerly accepted the challenge of becoming global citizens. Right To Play clubs popped up all over the city. Club members began educating other kids, parents and the public about the importance of sports and play in children's lives. They also started fund-raising campaigns, sold Right To Play t-shirts and mini red soccer balls, and organized Play Days.

"I doubt there's a kid in all of Surrey who doesn't know about Right To Play and what it does," said Robyn Cowie, Right To Play's Program Facilitator for Surrey.

Soon, local newspapers, businesses and citizens got behind the project too. Bus stops and streets were decorated with flags and posters encouraging everyone to accept the challenge to ensure that all children have the chance to play. And the Right To Play logo, "When Children Play, The World Wins," became the city's motto too. By the time the 2010 Winter Olympics started, Surrey was well on its way to meeting its goal of raising $200,000 for Right To Play.

Help at Home

The sense of community pride that came from Surrey citizens partnering with Right To Play is sure to go on for years to come.

Like many North American cities, Surrey is home to immigrant children who have come from countries faced with war, poverty and disease. Many of the same Right To Play games that are designed to help children cope with difficult situations in Africa, Asia and South America have been used in Surrey to help these children adjust to their new lives in Canada.

"At first, they were all pretty shy and we were told not to expect much from them," recalled Robyn Cowie. "So we just started playing some games and pretty soon, they were all running around, laughing and feeling

Kids in Surrey know about Right To Play and the work they do for children all over the world.

Credit: Gina McMurchy-Barber

Surrey, British Columbia jumped at the chance to make Right To Play its charitable partner during the 2010 Winter Olympics.

much more comfortable with us. We sat in a circle and asked them what their hopes and dreams were. At first things were pretty quiet, but soon [the children] started to open up. One girl told us she wanted to be a singer. With a little encouragement, she got up and sang for the group. Another boy said his dream was to grow up and become a good father. Well, that left me with a lump in my throat."

Today, Right To Play continues to make positive changes in the lives of children worldwide. The organization partners with Ministries of Education in developing curriculum and delivering programs. With the help of 13,000 trained local volunteer Coaches, Right To Play delivers its sports and play programs, as well as special events, to nearly one million disadvantaged children worldwide. Evidence is pouring in that shows progress is being made. School attendance has improved; there's also better learning ability, higher motivation and a greater sense of joy and well being.

Right To Play now runs a Junior Leader program that allows approximately 3,000 youth between the ages of eight and seventeen to learn leadership skills and take on active roles in their communities by leading other children in sports and play activities. These young leaders are gaining newfound confidence while building knowledge that will help them improve their own futures, as well as those of others.

A new generation of Right To Play junior leaders is taking an active role in teaching games to younger children in their communities.

The Next Challenge

While this might be the end of this book on Right To Play, it's not the end of the story. There are new chapters to be written and there's no reason you can't be part of them. You've read how kids like Mohamad, Esther, Yonas, John, and Cole and his teammates made a difference in the world. They didn't do it alone though. They were part of a bigger team—the Right To Play team.

The great civil rights leader Mahatma Gandhi knew that the steps to a better world started with children. He once said: "Be the change you wish to see in the world." What would it take for you and your friends to be world changers? How would you feel knowing you played a part in helping the most disadvantaged children become healthy and happy? There are infinite ways you can make a contribution—whether it's raising money or raising awareness. If you're feeling as if the task is too big, just remember what Yonas said: "I can do it!" And you will.

GLOSSARY

Athlete Ambassador: an Olympic or professional athlete who is committed to improving the lives of disadvantaged children by being a Right To Play spokesperson, educating children and raising funds.

Gender rules: expected behaviours and activities that are specific to males and females.

Learning to Play, Playing to Learn: Right To Play's free school program available to North American teachers to use in the classroom.

Live Safe, Play Safe: an education program that uses sport and play to teach HIV/AIDS awareness and prevention to youth.

LOOC: Lillehammer Olympic Organizing Committee organized Olympic Aid for the 1994 Winter Olympics.

Look After Yourself, Look After One Another: Right To Play's philosophy, which appears on all their red soccer balls and promotional material.

Olympic Aid: an awareness and fundraising organization conceived in 1992 by the Lillehammer Olympic Organizing Committee (LOOC).

Play Day: an organized event that brings children together to learn through games: Red Mind Ball games teach concentration and memory skills; Black Body Ball games focus on physical development; Blue Peace Ball games teach cooperation and teamwork; Yellow Spirit Ball games teach self-confidence and positive emotions; and Green Health Ball games focus on nutrition, hygiene and health.

SportHealth: Right To Play programs that focus on health issues.

SportWork: Right To Play programs that use sports and play to develop children's physical, social and emotional well being.

Volunteer Coach: a nurturing role model and member of a community who takes the Right To Play training in order to implement the programs with local children.

UNICEF: Right To Play has partnered with United Nations International Children's Emergency Fund for many projects worldwide.

United Nations: an international organization of independent states formed in 1945 to promote worldwide peace, cooperation and security for all people.

UN Convention on the Rights of the Child, Article 31: "States Parties recognize the right of the child to rest and leisure, to engage in play and recreational activities appropriate to the age of the child and to participate freely in cultural life and the arts."

United We Serve: a volunteering collective initiated by President Barack Obama in 2009 to engage citizens in an effort to improve their communities, countries and the world.

When Children Play, The World Wins: a Right To Play motto.

WHO: Right To Play has partnered with the World Health Organization for many projects.

INDEX

A
Afewerki, President Isaias, *17*
Al Hussein, HRH Princess Haya Bint, *24, 43*
Andersen, Hjalmar, *13*
Assaf, Mohamad, *24, 45-48*
Athlete Ambassador, *18, 25-27, 54*

B
Batter Up game, *11*
Black Body Ball games, *37, 54*
Blue Peace Ball games, *37, 54*

C
Cantelon, Cole, *8*
Cowie, Robyn, *51*

D
disability, *31-34*
Dybendahl, Trude, *13*

E
Esther, *40-42*

F
Frozen Beanbag game, *43*

G
Gebrselassie, Haile, *23, 24*
gender rules, *39, 54*
Green Health Ball games, *37, 54*
Gretzky, Wayne, *24, 49*

H
Hoffman, Ruth, *9*
homemade ball, *15, 20-22, 23*
Hughes, Clara, *24, 37*

J
Junior Leader, *52*

K
Koss, Johann Olav, *14-19, 54*

L
Laumann, Silken, *25*
Learning to Play, Playing to Learn program, *47, 54*
Lillehammer Olympic Organizing Committee (LOOC), *12, 54*
Live Safe, Play Safe program, *21-22, 54*

M
Mead, Margaret, *47*

N
Nsabimana, John, *20-22*

O
Obama, President Barack, *45*
Olympic Aid, *12-18, 54*

P
Pedersen, Cato Zahl, *13*
Play Day, *24, 29, 54*

R
Red Minds Ball games, *37, 54*
refugee camp, *14-18, 19, 20-22, 27-29*
Rumball, Jane, *27-29*

S
SportHealth, *37, 54*
SportWork, *37, 54*
Stone, Nikki, *26*

T
Tadesse, Yonas, *24, 31-34*
Tunnel Ball game, *35*
Tutu, Archbishop Desmond, *11*

U
Ulvang, Vegard, *13*
UN Convention of the Right of the Child, Article 31, *7, 54*
UNICEF, *17-18, 54*
United Nations (UN), *6, 33-34, 54*
United We Serve, *45, 54*

V
vaccination, *18, 39*
volunteer Coach, *29-30, 31-34, 54*
Volunteer Volleyball game, *49*
volunteering, *44-45, 46-48*

W
Whitfield, Simon, *24, 35*
World Health Organization (WHO), *18, 54*

Y
Yellow Spirit Ball games, *37, 54*

Z
Zaun, Gregg, *10*
Zigbu, Christopher, *30*

RESOURCES

Teacher Resource Guide: Learning to Play, Playing to Learn
Available by contacting Right To Play:

Right To Play International
65 Queen Street West
Thomson Building, Suite 1900. Box 64
Toronto, Ontario, M5H 2M5
Canada
Tel: +1 416 498 1922
Fax: +1 416 498 1942

Right To Play
Canadian National Office
65 Queen Street West
Thomson Building, Suite 1801, Box 64
Toronto, Ontario. M5H 2M5
Tel: +1 416 203 0190
Fax: +1 416 203 0189

US National Office
49 W. 27th Street
Suite 930
New York, NY 10001
Tel: +1 646 649 8280

For general information, volunteer opportunities or to make a donation, contact
info@righttoplay.com

REFERENCES

"Annual Report 2008," Right To Play International, info@righttoplay.com

"Convention on the Rights of the Child," Charter of the United Nations, Article 31, http://www2.ohchr.org/english/law/crc.htm

"Johann Olav Koss on The Hour with George Stroumboulopoulos," December 6, 2008, CBC video, http://www.cbc.ca

"Red Ball Reports," Right To Play International, http://www.righttoplay.com/international/news-and-media/Pages/Newsarticles/Redballreport

"Right To Play," last modified December 23, 2012, http://en.wikipedia.org/wiki/Right_To_Play

"Taking the Right To Play to Ethiopia," Resource Guide, February 28, 2007, http://newsinreview.cbclearning.ca/wp-content/uploads/2007/02/play.pdf

"Ugandan Little League team gets major thrill from Canadian squad's visit," January 18, 2012, The Star, http://www.thestar.com/sports/baseball/article/1117254--ugandan-little-league-team-gets-major-thrill-from-canadian-squad-s-visit

All Athlete Ambassador quotes taken from www.righttoplay.com.